One of These Is Not Like the Others

BARNEY SALTZBERG

NEAL PORTER BOOKS

HOLIDAY HOUSE / NEW YORK

Neal Porter Books

Text and illustrations copyright © 2020 by Barney Saltzberg
All Rights Reserved
HOLIDAY HOUSE is registered in the U.S. Patent and Trademark Office.
Printed and bound in October 2019 at Toppan Leefung, DongGuan City, China.
The artwork for this book was created using Adobe photoshop with a Wacom Centiq.
Book design by Jennifer Browne
www.holidayhouse.com
First Edition
1   3   5   7   9   10   8   6   4   2

Library of Congress Cataloging-in-Publication Data

Names: Saltzberg, Barney, author, illustrator.
Title: One of these is not like the others / Barney Saltzberg.
Description: New York : Holiday House, 2020. | "Neal Porter Books." |
Summary: "Points out the differences between subjects and celebrates
them"— Provided by publisher.
Identifiers: LCCN 2019010715 | ISBN 9780823445608 (hardcover)
Subjects: | CYAC: Difference (Psychology)—Fiction. | Individuality—Fiction.
Classification: LCC PZ7.S1552 On 2020 | DDC [E]—dc23
LC record available at https://lccn.loc.gov/2019010715

For Rabbi Mark
and Harriet,
who have created
a community
that embraces everyone
who walks through
the door.

One of these is not like the others.

And that's just fine with us.

One of these is not like the others.

But we can still be friends.

One of these is not like the others.

And that's the way we rock.

One of these is not like the others.

And that's the way we roll.

One of these is not like the others.

And that's the way we fly.

One of these is not like the others.

Because you can never
have too many hats.

One of these is not like the others.

What a nice surprise.

One of these is not like the others.

And the other three were delicious.

Some of us are a little different.

And that's the way we like it!